Backyard Girls Club

For girls everywhere.
To the backyard and beyond!

Copyright © 2019 by More Creative, LLC

ISBN 978-0-578-60296-7

Rachel Fisher
Backyard Girls Club / Rachel Fisher, Meet the Backyard Girls! They meet every day after school at the fort and do all kinds of magical everyday things like save the day, walk dogs and sell lemonade - just to name a few! Join them in their adventures as they dream, create, and learn that face-to-face and heart-to-heart friendships are the best thing you can ever have!

Library of Congress Control Number: 2019918380

Editing by Wendi Lewis
Front Cover image and illustrations by Nalin Crocker
Book design by Amye King

Printed and bound in the United States of America
Skinner Printing, Montgomery, Alabama

Published by More Creative, LLC
P.O. Box 240124
Montgomery, AL 36124

rachelbfisher.com

Contents

MEET THE GIRLS OF CHERRY BLOSSOM PLACE

ALLIE + EMMA

1

Emma and Allie rode in the backseat of their family car, following behind a moving truck full of their furniture and boxes of stuff. Emma hoped her books were safe in the gigantic truck. She listened to her parents talk about where the sofa would look best while her sister Allie sang a song she was making up. Both added to the nervous feeling growing in Emma's stomach — it felt like spaghetti noodles jumping in her tummy. She called this feeling "nervous noodles." It was the same feeling she got when she took a math test.

As their car followed the moving truck through the curved streets, Emma saw lots of green grass and kids playing outside. It was different from their old neighborhood where a busy street meant no playing ball in the front yard.

THEN IT HAPPENED.

The moving truck jolted around the corner, interrupting Emma's thoughts. Her eyes landed on the street sign: Cherry Blossom Place. The nervous noodles were now in Emma's throat. She noticed this road was shorter than the others in the neighborhood and had a curve at the end that made a circle.

Their parents told Emma and Allie that this kind of street was called a cul-de-sac. Emma counted the houses. One, two, three, four all the way to 12. Five homes on each side with two at the top of the circle. Theirs was situated where the street began to make a circle.

The nervous noodles in Emma's tummy grew tighter.

"I love it, I love it, I LOVE IT! How big is my room?! Do I have a closet big enough for my tutus?!" Allie giggled with excitement.

"Your rooms are both big enough for girls your age," their Mom replied. "But please wait until the movers unpack your boxes to get your tutus, Allie. And Emma, please don't go looking for your books. The nice men in the moving truck will unpack those for you, too."

"Yes, ma'am," replied Emma and Allie in harmony.

The moving truck came to a stop in front of their new house. It was a one-story house with pinkish brick and green shutters. The men driving the gigantic moving truck unloaded boxes. The two sisters jumped out of the car. Allie twirled in the driveway, but Emma's eyes landed on the house next door. A pair of eyes peered out from the window. The nervous noodles stopped jumping.

***

BANG! BANG! BANG!

Startled, Emma peeked around the corner of her new kitchen. A girl who looked to be her age stood at the back door holding an American Girl doll by the hair and banging on the door. Emma liked the American Girl doll. She did not like the banging. The girl started talking before Emma even opened the door.

"Hi! I'm your neighbor. My name is Ruthie. I like American Girl. Do you like American Girl? Do you have a sister, too? I love your house! The pinkish brick is fancy!" Ruthie let herself in and walked past Emma, talking all the way to the kitchen. She had dark brown hair and was tall like Emma. She had freckles and a gap between her front teeth and wore a pair of purple shorts with a multi-colored braided belt and a matching striped shirt.

"What color is your room? Mine is viiiiiiolehhhhht (Ruthie dragged the word out dramatically). I wanted to paint it lime green, but my mom said lime green looked like puke."

RUTHIE

"Mine is lime-gre..." Emma began. Ruthie kept talking and made her way to the kitchen counter.

"Are these Oreo cookies?" she asked with her hand in the bag.

"Yes, but..." Emma started to respond and tell Ruthie that her Mom did not let her eat more than one cookie a day. Before she could say a word, Ruthie clawed three Oreos out of the bag. She put them in her mouth all at once and mumbled,

"Wuff's yuh name, anywah?"

Emma told Ruthie her name. Allie came twirling into the kitchen wearing a tutu. Ruthie said she had a sister named Chrissy and continued her chatter.

"Ok, so now that we are best friends I think it's time to go meet the others!"

"Others?" asked Emma. She was confused about how Ruthie could declare them best friends after meeting less than five minutes ago. Even though it was strange to her, it felt good. Like she already belonged on Cherry Blossom Place.

"The other girls who live on the street!" exclaimed Ruthie. "There are three more plus me and Chrissy. You guys make seven! Oh, seven is a lucky number! This must mean something magic!" Ruthie grabbed Emma by the arm and pulled her outside. Allie followed behind, still twirling in her tutu.

"CHRISSSSSSYYYYYYY!" Ruthie yelled toward the backyard of her house. Her arm was still hooked onto Emma's.

Chrissy appeared from around the corner. Her strawberry hair swished left, right, left, right as she skipped toward the driveway where Emma, Ruthie, and a twirling Allie stood. Ruthie made the introduction.

"Chrissy, this is Emma and Allie. They're our new neighbors!"

Chrissy wore a lime green dress and wore socks with polka dots printed on them. She carried a popsicle in one hand and a sketchbook in the other.

Ruthie cut the introduction short and took off across the street toward a large two-story brick house with blue shutters and a garage. Emma, Allie, and Chrissy followed behind. Chrissy ate a popsicle. Allie twirled. Emma noticed her nervous noodles were gone.

Two girls ran out of the front door. One was taller than the other. They wore matching denim shorts and vests with white t-shirts and jelly shoes.

"This is Gabby and Sophie," said Ruthie. "They moved to Cherry Blossom Place last year. They have a pool!" Ruthie clapped her hands and jumped on her

Gabby + Sophie

tiptoes. She grabbed Emma's arm (again) and pulled her closer. "This is Emma and her sister Allie. They moved into the house across the street with pinkish brick and green shutters!"

"Nice to meet you!" said Gabby and Sophie together. They both had blonde curly hair. Gabby's hair was in a fancy French braid and Sophie's hair was pulled in a perfect ponytail.

Emma said it was nice to meet them, too. Allie curtsied.

"There's one more girl to meet," said Ruthie. "Her name is Mia. She lives three houses down from here." Ruthie led the way as the six girls skipped, walked, and twirled toward Mia's house. It was a red brick house with black shutters.

BANG! BANG! BANG!

Ruthie was at it again.

Mia's mother opened the door. "Hi, girls! Ruthie. Chrissy. Gabby. Sophie. It's nice to see you today!" She nodded her head at each of the girls as she said their name. "Ruthie, what did I tell you about banging on the door last time?"

"Oh, doggy darn it!" said Ruthie. "I'm sorry! These two sisters moved in next door today and I am sooooo excited for them to meet Mia!"

"Ok, sweetie," replied Mia's mother in a quiet

voice. "Let's just keep it down next time. Mr. Jimmy is taking his afternoon nap."

Mia came to the door and her mother walked back into the kitchen and told the girls to have fun. Mia was tall like Emma. She had curly dark hair and wore a sweatsuit with a bear doing ballet printed across the front.

"This is Mia," said Ruthie to Emma and Allie. "She's an only child, which is why she can sometimes be..."

"RUTHIE!" Gabby raised her voice. "That isn't nice or TRUE!" Gabby took the introduction from there and then they all sat down in a circle in Mia's front yard. Mia didn't seem bothered by Ruthie's almost-rude comment. Emma figured it might be kind of normal.

"Girls," said Ruthie in a proper tone of voice, "Emma and Allie make seven. You know what that means!"

"MAGIC!"

Ruthie, Chrissy, Gabby, Sophie, and Mia shouted in unison. They all began to giggle. Emma and Allie looked at each other and they giggled, too.

ACTIVITY

Get to Know Your Neighbors (or any new friends!)

Making new friends can be intimidating, especially if you're in a new school or neighborhood. Even if you aren't the new girl on the block, making friends is something you'll do for life, so you might as well rock at it!

Wondering how to make friends? It's easy. Just ask questions! You never know — you might become friends with someone you'd least expect!

Here are 10 questions to ask and learn more about the friends (and future friends!) in your life. Share them with a friend or two and see what you learn about each other. Take these questions to the lunchroom or to the playground at school and discover the new friends waiting to meet you!

1. What are 3 words you would use to describe yourself?

2. What is your favorite thing about yourself?

3. What do you love to do most in the world?

4. Who are the most important people in your life?

5. If you could transport yourself where would you go and why?

6. How would you spend your "dream day"?

7. Who is your hero?

8. What do you want to be when you grow up? Why?

9. What is the best gift you ever received?

10. Which food would like to eat endless amounts of?

A VISIT FROM SANTA

2

It was 80 degrees on Christmas, but Santa Claus still came to Cherry Blossom Place. Emma, Allie, Gabby, Sophie, and Mia huddled in the center of the cul-de-sac. They talked about what Santa brought them and traded candy they scooped from their stockings.

"I got pink walkie talkies!" said Emma as she traded her Snickers for Mia's Kit-Kat.

"Santa brought me ballet shoes!" said Mia as she took a bite of the Snickers bar.

"There was a unicorn backpack under the tree for me!" said Allie as she sprinkled M&M's into her hand.

"Santa brought me an easel for painting," said Gabby.

"I got a microphone to practice my singing!" said Sophie. Their parents didn't let them eat candy.

The girls looked toward Ruthie and Chrissy's house wondering why they weren't outside yet. Curious, they skipped across the street and up the driveway.

That's when they saw IT.

Right in the middle of Ruthie and Chrissy's backyard, stood a tall object cloaked in a plastic cover with a big, red bow on top. Before the girls could knock on the door, it flung open. Ruthie barreled toward the tall, bow-and-plastic covered Christmas mystery and shouted,

"FOOORRRRRTTTTTTTTTTT!!!!!"

As soon as the other girls realized what it was, they joined in the shouting and the excitement, too.

"How did Santa know this is what I wanted most in the whole wide world!?" asked Ruthie, wide-eyed. She tugged at the blue plastic cover and it fell to the ground revealing the most fantastic fort the girls ever saw. It had three levels connected by a ladder and a shiny flagpole at the top with a balcony, windows, and a flower box. There was even a slide!

The girls stared in wonder and their imaginations churned. Ruthie scurried up the ladder and pulled off the big, red bow and tossed it to the ground.

"I can pretend to be a princess and this is my castle," Ruthie declared from the top of the fort. "Or I can pretend to be a pioneer on the frontier! Or I could move into this thing! This is the best Christmas present ever! THANKS, SANTA!" Ruthie looked up to the blue sky and puffy clouds as she thanked Santa.

"The important question is, how did Santa fit this fort into his sleigh!?" asked Emma.

"Maybe he had it sent UPS," suggested Gabby. "My daddy uses UPS all the time for work."

"Maybe he snapped his fingers and it just appeared!" said Allie with a yelp.

"I think he got it from Home Depot," said Mia.

"I don't care how Santa got it here," said Ruthie. "You are all invited to my fort anytime you want. It's not just mine. It's OURS!"

The next morning, the girls climbed to the top of the fort and sat in a circle. It was a little cooler than the day before, so the girls scooted close together.

"Girls, I've been thinking," said Ruthie through chattering teeth. "What in God's green earth are we going to do with this magnificent fort?" (Ruthie often used big words and phrases she heard from her grandmother and said them in a very proper way).

"I read these books once," began Emma. "They were about some girls who had a club kind of thing and.."

"O! O! O! I've always wanted to be in a club!" said Sophie.

"Let her finish!" said Gabby, making wide eyes toward her sister.

Emma started again. "Well, there was this club

thingy, and they solved mysteries in their neighborhood and got awards and stuff." Emma shrugged her shoulders and looked down. She wasn't always confident in her ideas.

"My mom is in a club," said Mia. "It's for women who like to knit."

"My granny is in a club, too!" said Allie. "It's a club to play cards on a bridge."

"We can totally start a club!" said Ruthie. "I knew when Emma and Allie moved to our street, something magic would happen!"

"What should we call it?" asked Gabby. There was a long silence.

"The Club in the Fort!" exclaimed Chrissy.

"No, no," reprimanded Ruthie. "That's too BLAH. How about The Magic Seven Girls of the Neato Fort!?"

"Too long," said Gabby. Ruthie let out a huff. She didn't like it when her ideas weren't chosen. Emma looked up.

"I have an idea," Emma said with a slight grin. "What if we called ourselves The Backyard Girls Club?"

Smiles erupted on all their faces, except Ruthie's. She looked at Gabby to see what she would say.

"I love it!" said Gabby.

"Me too!" said Sophie.

"I mean, I guess that's a good name," said Ruthie. "Yeah, ok. I like it, too."

"The Backyard Girls Club it is!" exclaimed Mia.

The seven girls who lived at the end of the cul-de-sac on Cherry Blossom Place were sure they had the best idea ever. Now they had to decide the important things. Like who would be president.

ACTIVITY

How to Bake Magic Cookie Bars

Emma and Allie's granny taught the Backyard Girls how to make her famous Magic Cookie Bars when she came for Christmas. Follow the recipe below (with adult supervision, of course!) and enjoy this magical treat! Be sure to make extra. You'll want to share!

Weren't these from you, Ann? They're just delicious!

Magic Cookie Bars

½ C margarine
1½ C graham cracker crumbs
1 can (14 oz.) Eagle Brand sweetened condensed milk (not evap.)
1 pkg. (6 oz.) semi-sweet chocolate morsels
1 can (3½ oz. = 1⅓ C) flaked coconut
1 C chopped nuts

Preheat oven to 350°. In 13" x 9" baking pan, melt margarine in oven. Sprinkle crumbs over margarine; mix together and press into pan. Pour condensed milk evenly over crumbs. Top evenly with remaining ingredients; press down firmly.

Bake 25-30 min. or until lightly browned. Cool thoroughly before cutting. Store loosely covered at room temp. (Makes 24 bars)

~*~*CLUB notes~*~*~

BACKYARD
~GIRLS CLUB~

MADAM PRESIDENT

3

The girls sat cross-legged in Emma and Allie's driveway eating chocolate chip cookies and drawing on the sidewalk with chalk. Gabby talked about her day at school. Since Gabby was the oldest, her stories about school were always the coolest.

"Today we had elections for student council," said Gabby.

"What's that?" asked Mia.

"It's like a club," replied Gabby. "But for school. Today, we voted on a president, secretary, and treasurer!"

"So, what do those people do if they win the election?" asked Ruthie. "Do they get to make the rules? Like the real President?"

"It's not exactly like that," said Gabby. "The president is like the leader of all the students. The secretary takes notes at the student council meetings when they talk about things like school lunches. The treasurer keeps up with the money the school makes from bake sales, performances and stuff like that."

Gabby said the girl who won president had a slogan to the tune of a Taylor Swift song and the boy who won secretary told everyone he would bring donuts to school every Friday morning.

Ruthie stood up, flung her arms out to her side, and said, "I've always wanted to be president of something. I think I would make a good one. I'm very reliable."

"I've always wanted to be a princess of something," sighed Allie. "But my mom said it isn't a real job."

"Yes-huh!" said Sophie. "Princess Kate has a real job!" Allie said she would tell her mom what Sophie said and drew crowns with a piece of yellow chalk on the driveway.

Gabby cleared her throat, "I've been thinking, and I think if we are going to be a real club, we need to have a president!"

"Does this mean whoever is president of the Backyard Girls Club has to boss us around?" asked Chrissy. "Because I get bossed around a lot already."

"No!" said Gabby. "The president of the Backyard Girls Club should never want to boss people around. Instead, our president should come up with fun activities for us to do, make sure we are all kind to each other, and think of ways for us to help our neighbors!"

"The president should also be close to the fort since I think that's where we should meet," said Ruthie. "The president needs to be able to get to the headquarters fast if there is a problem or anything."

"Are you saying that because the fort is in your backyard?" asked Mia.

"No," said Ruthie as she sat back down in the circle. "I'm saying it because I think it's important! The real President sleeps in the White House and meets with important people at the White House, so I think that's saying something pretty doggy-darn it important!"

Gabby suggested they make a ballot. She explained it would have President, Secretary, and Treasurer listed at the top. If anyone wanted to run for office, they should write their name under the job they wanted. Most everyone said Gabby should run for president.

Ruthie listed her name on the president list, too. "Since the fort is in my backyard and all," she said.

Emma was the only one who wrote her name down for secretary. She liked to write, so she figured it would be a fun job. Mia wrote her name down for treasurer. She was good at math.

Sophie suggested that Gabby and Ruthie give a speech the next day to explain why they thought they should be president. Everyone thought that was a good idea.

The next day, Gabby arrived at the fort with a poster with some writing in pink and purple glitter. She wore a purple, pink, and green striped shirt and a skirt. Ruthie was already at the fort when the rest of the girls arrived. She somehow managed to bring a desk up the wooden ladder and taped an American flag to the wall. Papers were stacked on her desk, and she wore her mother's blazer over polka-dotted overalls.

The girls gathered in a circle, as usual. Ruthie's desk was at the top of the circle. The American flag hung over their heads

"It feels like we're at my school," whispered Sophie to Allie. "Are we about to say the Pledge of Allegiance?"

"It's part of my campaign!" said Ruthie, overhearing her.

Emma called the girls to attention. Since she was secretary, she brought a notebook to the fort. It was pink and sparkly with Backyard Girls Club written on the front.

"This is the Pink Sparkly Notebook," said Emma. "This is where we will write all of our secrets and

passwords and important club thingies." The girls
loved the notebook.

"Ok, it's now time to hear from both of our pres-
idential candidates," she continued. "Gabby, you go
first. You have one minute to tell us why you would
make the perfect President of the Backyard Girls
Club."

Gabby stood up and placed her poster against
the wooden wall. In pink and purple glittery letters,
she wrote, "Gabby 4 Backyard Girls Club President

— Let's Have Fun!" Her perfect ponytail bounced as she began to talk.

Gabby told the girls she wanted to be president because she was experienced at being a leader. She reminded them she was president of the art club at school, good at solving arguments, and making sure everyone felt included. She promised to let everyone take turns in coming up with activities.

"As President," said Gabby, "I promise to make our club fun for all of us forever!"

Ruthie was up next. She jumped up and buttoned her mother's blazer. She sat down in the chair behind the desk and cleared her throat.

"My fellow Backyard Girls," Ruthie began. She was reading from the papers stacked on top of the desk. The girls stared up at Ruthie as she continued.

"Today, we have gathered together to make a decision. I hope you will make the right one. The Backyard Girls Club is a club for every girl, but especially for the girls who love the backyard and forts. Especially this fort you are sitting in now. As the owner of the fort, it only makes sense you vote for me as president. If it wasn't for the fort, who knows if we would have a Backyard Girls Club in the first place?!" Ruthie talked longer than one minute and ended her speech with, "To the backyard and beyond!"

When Ruthie was finished, Emma announced that it was time to vote. She passed out pieces of construction paper with Gabby and Ruthie's name written on them with a small box drawn next to their name. Emma told the girls to check the box next to the name of the girl they wanted to vote for, fold up the paper, and drop it in the orange mixing bowl she took from her mom's kitchen cabinet. After a few minutes, the votes were in. It was time to count.

Emma put votes for Gabby in one pile and votes for Ruthie in the other.

"The votes are in," said Emma. "Let's give a round of applause for our president: Gabby!" Everyone clapped and cheered. Except for Ruthie.

"Aw, come on, Ruthie!" said Allie. "You gave a good speech! And I really liked your slogan!"

"Yea!" said Gabby. "How about we use your slogan as our official Backyard Girls Club slogan?" Ruthie's frown quickly turned into a smile.

"REALLY?" said Ruthie. "You would do that?"

"Of course!" said Gabby. "I think we should include everybody's good ideas."

"I think Ruthie should be Vice President!" said

Mia. Ruthie bounced on her tippy toes at the thought of being vice president.

"Yea, and you pulled a desk up the fort ladder!" said Sophie. "You must be really strong!"

Ruthie was so excited she couldn't help but jump up on the desk and announce, "Gabby, we are lucky to have you as our Backyard Girls Club President. I am happy to accept your nomination as Vice President! To the backyard and beyond!"

The girls all stood up and raised their voices together,

"TO THE BACKYARD! AND BEYOND!"

Gabby said the first thing they needed to do was come up with three rules and a secret password. Gabby said the password could be something silly.

"How about Lollipop Socks?" asked Chrissy. The girls giggled. They knew Chrissy loved to wear crazy socks and it was no surprise that she was wearing socks with lollipops on them that day.

"Perfect! We will say the password every time we come into the fort," said Gabby.

"And you must pinky promise you won't tell it to anyone," said Ruthie. "The password is our magic code!"

As for the three rules of the Backyard Girls Club, those were easy to decide on. They wrote them on the wall of the fort with a pink sparkly marker that matched the Pink Sparkly Notebook:

1. Always be kind!
2. No idea is a bad idea!
3. Treat everyone how you want to be treated.

They also added one more rule: P.S. No Boys Allowed.

ACTIVITY

3 Things You Can Do With Sidewalk Chalk

Getting creative with sidewalk chalk is one of the Backyard Girls' favorite things to do. It's the best way to liven up any day! All you need is a driveway or sidewalk and some chalk. Voila! You have a canvas for anything you can think of! Here are some the Backyard Girls' favorite things to do with their sidewalk chalk on Cherry Blossom Place.

1. **Body Outline Trace**

   Divide up into groups of two. Take turns laying down on the driveway in different positions then draw around each other's shapes. When you're done, fill and color the outline with a face, features and clothes. Get extra creative and give each one a theme like princess, astronauts and even President of the United States...just to name a few!

2. **Starry Night**

   Print out several pictures of famous art masterpieces that have simple lines and shapes. Let everyone choose one and try their hand at re-creating the work of art with your side walk chalk. Who knows?! You might be the next Van Gogh!

3. **Sidewalk Chalk Message**

   Use your sidewalk chalk to make your neighbors smile! Write or draw a message with large letters along the sidewalk where your neighbors will see it. It's a fun way to bring a bright spot to someone's day!

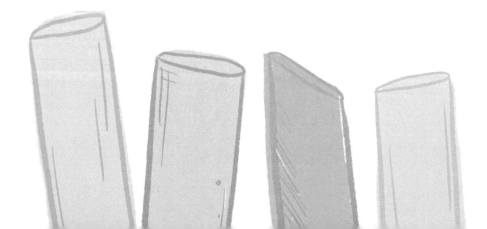

~*~*CLUB notes~*~*

BACKYARD
~GIRLS CLUB~

THE BOY NEXT DOOR

4

Matt Miller lived next door to Mia. His parents were science professors and his older sister went to college. Matt was the only boy on Cherry Blossom Place. Most days, he wore baggy jeans and a t-shirt featuring his favorite comic or Star Wars character. His brown hair always looked wet, but it was just his hair gel.

Matt rode a neon green scooter with fire-breathing dragons painted on it up and down, up and down Cherry Blossom Place every day after school. The sound of his left foot pounding the pavement and the "CLICK-CLACK" as he sped over the gaps in the sidewalk gave the warning: Matt was coming.

When Matt rode his dragon scooter around the cul-de-sac, he would do tricks. He would jump off the curb into the air, turn his scooter in circles, and grunt:

"HIIII-YA!"

Matt was also getting his orange belt in karate.

One afternoon while the girls were playing hopscotch down the sidewalk, they saw Matt.

"Look! There goes Matt on his dragon-y scooter," announced Sophie. They watched as Matt did a new trick where he jumped off the curb into the air and turned in two circles before the wheels touched the pavement.

"He only wants attention," said Gabby. "Don't stare at him." Matt and Gabby went to the same school, but she had never talked to him.

None of the girls had talked to Matt Miller, but they heard the stories about him. Gabby said a girl at school slapped Matt across the face because he stole her glitter pencils and sold them at the school supply store. Chrissy said she heard he kept an alien as a pet. "I hear he keeps it in an aquarium in his room," she said. "My cousin told me his dad captured it when they went on a family vacation to Arizona."

Their storytelling was interrupted when Ruthie and Chrissy's dog, a white-haired poodle named Fairy, ran to the end of the driveway and barked, as ferociously as a poodle can, in Matt's direction.

Fairy's bark startled Matt. He toppled off his scooter and landed on the asphalt in the middle of the cul-de-sac. The girls stared, wondering what to do. Matt was 12. His height, along with the dragons on his scooter, made him seem like a giant to them.

"Yikes. Should we go help him?" asked Chrissy.

"No! Our rules say no boys allowed!" said Ruthie through her teeth.

"But he fell off his scooter!" whispered Emma. "Shouldn't we at least make sure he's okay?"

"Our rules also say to help our neighbors," Gabby reminded them.

Conflicted, the girls turned and watched as Matt stood up, dusted off his jeans, and looked toward them.

"Are they just gonna stand there?" Matt wondered. He needed one of them to rescue him from his biggest fear.

"RUFFFFF! RUFFFF!! GRRRRUFFFFFF!" Fairy inched closer to a frozen Matt Miller.

"That's right, Fairy!" shouted Ruthie from the sidewalk. "Boys equal BARK!"

Mia felt terrible for Matt and didn't care what Ruthie said. She thought Gabby had a good point. It was more important to help Matt than to stick to the P.S. Rule. She started down the driveway even though Ruthie kept shouting out the P.S. rule:

"No, Mia! No boys allowed!"

"Hi Matt, I'm Mia," she said as she walked closer. "I live next door to you. Are you OK?"

Matt couldn't speak. He just stared at Fairy.

"Matt? Are you hurt?" asked Mia. "My mom is a nurse. She can help if you are!"

Matt's eyes darted away from Fairy and onto Mia's face.

"Nnn- nnn-no just my, my, scoot- scooter," Matt stuttered. "And I, I, I- d-d-don't like…"

"Matt, you don't need to be afraid of Fairy," said Mia. She leaned in close so Ruthie wouldn't hear and whispered, "She's just a miniature poodle."

Matt let out a deep breath as Fairy's bark turned to a yap. Ruthie's mom came outside.

"FAIRY!" Mrs. Sandy hollered from the front porch. "What is this?! Matt Miller! Are you ok?!" Mrs. Sandy hurried to the sidewalk and scooped up Fairy in one arm. "Matt, do I need to call your mother?"

"No, ma'am," said Matt. "I, I, I, I'm okay. It's just that your dog — I don't…"

"Well, I am taking her inside. You don't have to worry about Fairy."

"BUT MOMMMM," said Ruthie. "Fairy is our mascot! And besides, she keeps boys away from our club. Obviously!"

"Ruthie, we cannot have Fairy be responsible for people hurting themselves. Fairy will be inside. You girls can keep playing until the streetlights come on. Matt, you can ride your scooter down anytime. The girls and I will make sure Fairy is out of your way." Matt nodded and said thank you.

Mia walked Matt toward the other girls. He carried his scooter in one hand and combed his fingers through his hair with the other.

"I know we said no boys allowed, but I think we

should introduce ourselves," said Mia.

"Golly, you're really tall!" said Allie.

"Is it true you stole glittery pencils?" asked Sophie.

"And that you have an alien for a pet?" added Allie.

Matt was used to people asking him weird questions, so he changed the subject.

"What do you guys do down here every day? I always see you in that fort thing sitting in a circle."

The girls looked at each other. Should they tell him what they did? Who they were?

"We have a club," said Gabby. "It's called the Backyard Girls Club."

"Oh, hey, I know you," said Matt. "You go to my school."

"Yeah, I know," she said. "I'm Gabby." The other girls followed Gabby's lead and introduced themselves to Matt. Ruthie went last.

"So, Matt, we have a rule," said Ruthie. She crossed her arms across her chest and tapped one foot. "It's called the no-boys-allowed rule."

"We also have another rule," chimed in Gabby. "We want to help our neighbors, and even though you are a boy, we thought helping you off the middle of the street was more important."

"Gee, thanks," Matt replied. "But Mia is the real hero." Matt looked at Mia and smiled. "Since you helped me and all," he said to her. Mia blushed. "I know it's weird, but I am kind of afraid of dogs."

"I am, too!" said Allie. "Big ones, though. Not small ones like Fairy."

Ruthie was still tapping her foot. "Ok, Matt, it was good to meet you and all, and I'm sorry about your scratched-up dragon scooter, but I think it's time for you to go. We have secret club things to do."

"Oh, yeah, ok sure," said Matt.

Mia told Matt bye and that she would see him around. She didn't think he was so bad after all. Maybe what people said about Matt wasn't true.

"Thanks for your help, Mia," said Matt. He turned around and started down the driveway on his scratched-up scooter, his left foot pounding the pavement. Matt was on his way home. For now.

ACTIVITY

3 Ways To Be Kind

It's easy to think you know someone because of what other people say about them. But what if those things aren't true? Like what if Matt Miller doesn't have an alien for a pet and never stole glittery pencils in the first place?! That's why it's always important to be kind to everyone. Even the person you think is a meanie. Here are 3 ways you can be kind to anyone, anywhere, anytime.

1. **Smile at them.**

   A smile is the best way to communicate kindness. A smile can make someone who is having a bad day feel better and you'll feel happy, too! **Who is someone who needs a smile?**

   _____

2. **Look for the person with no one to play with.**
   See that girl standing by herself? Is that boy eating lunch alone? Does she usually get picked last for the team? Make it your job to show them some love! Invite her to play with you and your friends, take your lunch and sit with that boy, pick her for the team first. Your kindness can change someone's world! **Who are some people who need to feel loved by you and your friends? What can you invite them to do? Go do it!**

   _____

   _____

3. **Write a note.**

   Write a note to someone who needs encouragement. It doesn't have to be long! Make a card out of paper, stickers, glitter or anything you find and send it to them in the mail! You can even put it on their door, desk or sneak it in their lunch box. If you want to have a little extra fun, don't sign your name. Let them wonder who their random act of kindness came from! **Who needs encouragement? A kind word? A laugh?**

   _____

Send kindness their way!

~*~*CLUB noTES~*~*

BACKYARD
~GiRLs CluB~

THE BACKYARD GIRLS TO THE RESCUE

5

It was the first day of Spring Break. The top of the fort was the best place to be — at least for the Backyard Girls. From there they could see new houses being built on the street behind Ruthie's house, two lakes, walking paths, and a wooded area they called the Magic Forest. They never ventured into the Magic Forest beside the lake. Their parents said they weren't allowed to cross the ditch without permission and definitely not allowed near the lakes or woods without an adult. Neighbors said alligators were in the lake and coyotes in the forest.

"Since it's the first day of Spring Break we should do something fun to celebrate," suggested Ruthie.

The girls agreed and bounced ideas around:

"My mom can make brownies!" said Allie.

"We could watch movies and eat ice cream with the brownies Allie and Emma's mom makes!" said Mia.

"Oooo or we could do makeovers!" said Sophie.

"Or," began Gabby, "we could do all of those things and have a spend-the-night party!"

"Yes! I love that idea!" Ruthie shouted. Ruthie always liked Gabby's ideas. She started down the ladder and announced she would go ask her mom if they could spend the night at her house. The girls were giggly at the thought of a spend-the-night party.

Before she made it down the ladder, Ruthie looked up at the girls with wide eyes and a smile. She had an idea.

"Oh my goodness, girls! What if we spent the night in the fort!?"

"Sleep outside? In here?" asked Sophie.

"What if the alligators come? Or the coyotes? The Magic Forest is not very far away!" said Emma.

"Not gonna happen," said Gabby. "Plus, we can go inside if we need to!"

The girls gave in to Gabby's reassurance. Ruthie scurried down the ladder, ran into the house and reappeared a minute later.

"My mom said yes!" yelled Ruthie as she ran toward the fort. "She just said you all need to go ask your parents."

The girls cheered and ran back to their houses to ask their parents if they could spend the night at the fort. Their parents gave a hesitant yes, convinced that the girls wouldn't make it past 8:00 before they came inside to sleep.

The girls gathered at the fort after dinner. Emma and Allie brought brownies with chocolate chips and fudge. Mia brought two games: Jenga and Monopoly. Ruthie brought a basket full of candy, soda, and chips. Sophie brought a box of makeup from her mom's bathroom cabinet, and Gabby brought magazines, scissors, tape, glue, and construction paper to make collages.

"This is the best idea I've ever had!" said Ruthie as she spread her Cinderella sleeping bag next to Gabby's on the second level of the fort.

Emma and Mia claimed the top level where they could sleep under the stars. Sophie, Allie, and Chrissy made a pallet on the ground level of the fort.

"We want to be down here so we can run if a coyote comes," said Allie.

"Um, that's not going to work," said Ruthie. "You basically would be the coyote's first stop." The three younger girls screamed, grabbed their stuff and moved to the second level.

After they got settled, the girls played games and ate brownies, candy, and chips. Gabby French-braided everyone's hair and Sophie passed around her mom's red lipstick that she took from her drawer.

"It's called Fire Truck Red," said Sophie as she read the name off the bottom of the stick.

"Sophie, did you take that from mom's cabinet? You're gonna get grounded!"

Sophie shrugged her shoulders and passed the lipstick to Chrissy.

It was getting late and the only noise they heard was the wind whispering through the trees. Occasionally, a coyote's howl echoed through the air, but it was far away. At least that's what Gabby told them. When it got late, the girls decided to sleep on the second level of the fort together and everyone fell sound asleep with their French-braided hair and red lipstick still

intact. Except for Emma. She took her sleeping bag to the third level, where the flag flew, to look at the stars. After a few minutes, she noticed an orange reflection on the flagpole. Curious, she looked across the ditch. That's when she spotted it.

Emma ran down the stairs shouting:

"FIRE! FIRE!"

The girls shot up from their sleeping bags with their eyes half-closed, yawning and asking a collective, "Huh?! What?"

"There is a fire! Across the ditch! One of the new houses being built!" said Emma, out of breath.

"Ok, we have to call 9-1-1!" said Gabby as she jumped out of her sleeping bag and slid into her puppy dog slippers.

"Guys, we need to stop, drop and roll," said Chrissy.

"No!" said Ruthie. "We need to go inside and call 9-1-1 right this second!" Ruthie ran inside and grabbed the phone. "Guys, I've got this," she said as she dialed the number and the other girls looked on. "This is just like on TV."

"9-1-1 What's your emergency?" the operator asked.

"Hi, yes, this is Ruthie on Cherry Blossom Place. I am calling to say there is a house on fire across the ditch!"

"What street is the emergency on?"

"The street across the ditch!" Ruthie repeated.

"Give me the phone!" said Gabby. She delivered Girl Scout Cookies and knew the streets by name.

"Hi, 9-1-1, this is Gabby speaking. The fire is on Willow Tree Road."

"Thank you, young lady. The fire department is on their way."

A few minutes later, fire trucks appeared on Willow Tree Road. The girls stood at the ditch and watched the firefighters spray the burning house with water hoses. Soon, the fire was out and the girls cheered and clapped.

"Thank you, Mr. Firemen!" they shouted across the ditch.

The fire chief and a fireman walked toward the ditch. "Are you all the girls who called 9-1-1?" they asked.

"Yes, I am!" said Ruthie as she raised her hand in the air.

"We all did," said Gabby, stepping forward.

"Well, girls, you all need to know what a great thing you did here tonight."

The girls looked at each other and smiled; their French braids still perfect and fire truck red lipstick still on bright.

"If you had not seen the fire and called 9-1-1, the neighbors' houses could have caught on fire, too."

"Well, we are the Backyard Girls Club," said Ruthie. "We are very reliable." The Fire Chief and fireman chuckled.

"Well, Backyard Girls Club, we want to give you an award for your service this evening." The Fire Chief reached inside the pocket of his jacket and pulled out seven shiny gold medals that said, "Good Citizen Award."

"I present to you, the Backyard Girls Club, Good Citizen medals for your service tonight! You all saved your fellow neighbors from a hazardous fire."

"Oh, my goodness! Oh, my goodness!" shouted Ruthie as she jumped on her tiptoes.

Emma put her hands over her mouth and Mia gasped. Sophie, Chrissy, and Allie linked arms jumping up and down.

"Thank you, thank you, thank you!" they said with yelps of joy and laughter. They each took their medals and put them around their necks. They were proud.

By now, their parents were outside, the commotion from the fire trucks waking them up. They were worried, of course, and started asking the firemen a whole lot of questions.

"You don't need to worry," the Fire Chief assured them. "Your daughters all saved the day!" Or more like the night!"

The girls told their parents about how they saw the fire and called 9-1-1 and didn't even cross the ditch. They fell asleep proud of how they saved their neighborhood. The next day, they brainstormed about all the ways they could help their neighbors on Cherry Blossom Place. The fun was just beginning.

ACTIVITY

How to Make a Collage

What you need:
- A stack of old magazines
- A pair of scissors
- A glue stick
- Construction paper

The Backyard Girls love to make collages! Here are some simple steps you can follow to make collages of your own. Don't be afraid to get creative! There are no rules to make a collage!

Step One: Flip through the old magazines and find images that you think are pretty, interesting or that you just like. The images you pick can have a common theme, or not. Cut out a lot of images and don't worry about using them all…the more the merrier!

Step Two: Get creative! Don't just cut squares or rectangles on the page. Instead, follow the lines in the photograph. For example, if you are cutting an image that has a car in it, cut the shape of the car out. It will give you more room to add more photographs!

Step Three: Now, it's time for the real fun to begin! Pick out a piece of construction paper in a color you like. Begin gluing your favorite images onto the construction paper in whatever shape, form or fashion you want until the entire page is covered with images.

Step Four: Share your collage with your friends and see how they created their own! You can learn a lot about your friends by seeing what they put on their collage!

Bonus: Want to add more to your magazine collage? Add sequins, old buttons, newspaper, glitter or even write on your collage with colored markers and pens! This is your way of expressing yourself!

~*~*CLuB noTes~*~*

BACKYARD
~GiRLs CLuB~

THE DOG WALKER GIRLS

6

One afternoon, Emma and Allie brought a surprise to the fort. It was a cute, cuddly puppy they adopted from the humane shelter.

"What an adorable nose!" said Gabby.

"Aw, I love his eyes!" said Sophie.

"She is so friendly!" said Mia as the puppy licked her face.

"Enjoy your puppy while you can," said Ruthie. "Because it will get big and bark at boys on scooters and your mom will make her stay inside and never come out to play." (Ruthie was still sore about what happened with Matt Miller).

"Ruthie, I'm sorry about what happened to Fairy," said Emma. She cuddled the golden-haired puppy she named Ivey close to her chest. "Maybe we should train her!"

"We could be like — like, dog trainers!" shouted Allie. "My parents said we have to train Ivey, so let's train Fairy, too!"

"See?" said Emma, "We are teaching Ivey to walk on a leash!" Emma placed Ivey on the grass and clipped a hot pink leash to Ivey's collar. "Ok, Ivey! Let's walk!" Ivey trotted alongside Emma and wagged her tail.

"Wow!" said Ruthie. "If Fairy can learn to walk on a leash maybe she can be our mascot again!"

"We can have two mascots!" said Mia.

"Fairy will always be our number one mascot, Mia," said Ruthie. "Ivey is second."

Ruthie ran inside her house and reappeared a few moments later carrying Fairy. She clipped a lime green leash with dog bones printed on it onto Fairy's collar and walked Fairy around the backyard. Fairy didn't bark, but she pulled on the leash a little.

"Don't pull!" yelled Ruthie. The girls giggled.

After a few minutes, Fairy seemed to like walking on a leash. They clapped for Fairy and decided to take both dogs for a walk down Cherry Blossom Place.

"This is fun!" said Emma.

"Yea, I like walking dogs!" said Sophie.

"We should walk everyone's dogs!" said Allie as she ran ahead of the group.

"What if we walked our neighbors' dogs, too?" suggested Gabby. "We could walk them around the block and play with them! We could start our own Backyard Girls Club business!"

The girls agreed that this was the best idea ever. They raced back to the fort and collected construction paper, glitter, and markers to make flyers and business cards.

THE BACKYARD GIRLS:
~ LeT uS WaLk YoUr DoG!*~*
$1 A DOG

**Come see us at the fort after school
and we will walk your dogs!**

The girls knocked on every door on Cherry Blossom Place and passed out their fliers and business cards. Their neighbors were happy to see the Backyard Girls. Especially after they saved the neighborhood from catching on fire.

"This a grand idea!" said Ms. Anne when they came to her house. She was an old lady with a cat and lived next door to Ruthie and Chrissy. "I'll let you walk my Tabitha anytime." Ms. Anne sometimes thought her cat was a dog.

The next day, the Backyard Girls had an unexpected surprise. Every neighbor brought their dogs to the fort. There were 15 dogs in all, including Fairy and Ivey.

There were small dogs, medium-sized dogs, and a few big dogs. They were barking and jumping and running around the fort. Ruthie took charge. She climbed to the top of the fort and called everyone to attention.

"Hi, neighbors! Thanks for coming to the fort! We are the Backyard Girls. We are SOOOO excited to walk your dogs. We are professionals!" Ruthie continued. "Do we need to know anything about any of these doggies?"

THE BACKYARD GIRLS CLUB
~ LeT uS WaLk YoUr DoG!*~*
$$1 A DoG
COME + SEE US AT THE FORT AND WE WILL WALK YOUR DOG

"My pup Percy has arthritis, so he's a little slow on the leash but needs the exercise," said Mr. Bob.

"My dog Scooter sometimes stops to smell bushes, but you just yank him away," said Ms. Susan.

Other neighbors told the girls their dogs wouldn't give them any trouble and what to do if they did. Also, Ms. Anne brought her cat.

Emma took notes about each of their new customers in the Pink Sparkly Notebook.

After a few minutes, the girls had the dogs on their leashes. Allie, Sophie, and Chrissy decided they would walk Fairy, Ivey, and Mr. Bob's dog with arthritis. The other dogs were in the hands of Gabby, Emma, Mia, and Ruthie.

"Ok, we have 12 dogs," said Mia, "and four of us. That means each of us can walk three dogs. Mia was good at math.

Ruthie took hold of a Dalmatian named Spot, a Labrador named Scooter, and a Great Dane called Jazzy.

Mia walked three Springer Spaniels named Bess, Jess, and Tess.

Emma walked a sweet collie named Missy, a Husky named Snowball and a basset hound named Molly.

Gabby walked a terrier named Rex, a Saint Bernard called Paddington, and a Golden Retriever named Lady.

Ms. Anne's cat walked by herself on the other side of the street.

The Backyard Girls were proud. They were doing it! Walking dogs and helping their neighbors all while making a few bucks. As they walked, they discussed what they would do with their money.

That's when it happened.

Allie, Sophie, and Chrissy walked too close to Ruthie and the dogs she was walking. Allie tripped and the leash holding Fairy left her hand.

"RUFFFF RUFFFF RUFFFF," Fairy ran toward Ruthie and the big dogs she was walking.

"Oh, doggy-darn it!" shouted Ruthie. "Fairy, NO!" Then Ruthie ran into Emma. Emma ran into Mia. And Mia ran into Gabby.

And all seven girls, 15 leashes, and dogs collided. The girls screamed, pushed, and shouted, while the dogs barked, whined, and scurried every which way.

Fairy ran further away and the bigger dogs were wagging their tails in the girls' faces and jumping, making it impossible to figure out which leash belonged to which dog.

"This is a disaster!" shouted Gabby above the yelps coming from the dogs and other girls.

"I only tripped!" shouted Allie. "I'm the worst dog walker girl ever!"

By now, all the leashes were tangled together. Eventually, they gave up and collapsed in the middle of the sidewalk. Tabitha, Ms. Anne's cat, watched from a distance. Then, the tears came.

"We told them we were professionals!" cried Ruthie. "This situation is not a professional one!"

Emma tried to reassure everyone, but everyone else started crying too.

"Now my parents definitely won't let me get a dog of my own!" sobbed Mia.

"I'm never walking dogs again!" whined Sophie.

The neighbors, drawn out of their homes by the yelping, yelling, and barking, came outside. They gently told the girls to back away. Mr. Bob helped untangle the leashes. The neighbors took their dogs, thanked the girls for their efforts, and walked back to their houses.

"We only wanted to keep being good citizens!" said Emma. "I guess we should just stick to walking our own dogs now."

The Backyard Girls went back to the fort, counted their money, and decided to try a lemonade stand next time.

ACTIVITY

How to Start Your Own Backyard Girls Club Neighborhood Business

With the right tools, you can start a neighborhood business, too! Here are some ways to have fun helping your neighbors and make a few dollars for your Backyard Girls Club or to give to a charity or someone in need!

1. **Brainstorm! Decide what kind of business you want to start!** Ask yourselves a few questions: What are the needs on our street? Do people need dog walkers? A lemonade stand to cool off from the summer heat? Cookies? Babysitters? The list is endless!

2. **Decide how much to charge!** Ask the adults in your life to help you come up with a price for your services. It doesn't need to be much!

3. **Make flyers or business cards and spread the word!** You just need some paper, markers, pens and maybe some glitter! Pass out your flyers or cards to your neighbors and tell them about what you hope to help them with or provide them with and how they can get in touch with you.

4. **Decide what you want to do with the money you make from your neighborhood business.** Do you want to save it for your next big idea? Give it to a local charity or someone in need? Ask a parent or adult to help you count, sort and decide what to do with the money you make from your Backyard Girls Club Business!

5. **Have fun learning how to work together!**

~*~*CLUB notes~*~*

BACKYARD
~GIRLS CLUB~

THE BEST FRIEND NECKLACE

7

A small half of a golden heart that said "Best" dangled from Gabby's neck. Emma never noticed it before. Then she remembered how they celebrated Gabby's birthday the week before, and everyone gave Gabby a gift.

Emma and Allie gave Gabby a glittery baton with pom poms. Mia gave Gabby a notepad with her name and butterflies printed on it. Sophie gave her sister a pair of purple, sparkly tennis shoes and Chrissy gave Gabby a hair bow. But Ruthie didn't give Gabby a present — yet.

The Backyard Girls Club meeting began and Chrissy showed everyone how to make a kite out of tissue paper. Emma looked around, her eyes glancing at everyone's neck. Emma knew someone had to be wearing the other half of the heart necklace.

It didn't take long for Emma to spot the other half hanging from Ruthie's neck. Her white shirt made it stand out.

"Did any of the other girls notice the necklaces?"

thought Emma. She watched Ruthie pull at her necklace and twirl it around in her hands. "She is trying to get everyone to notice," Emma thought.

"Hey, Ruthie," interrupted Mia, "What's that thing around your neck?" Emma was glad Mia spoke up.

"Oh, this golden thingy with a pink stone?" asked Ruthie, pretending not to know what she was talking about. "It's just a necklace I bought at the mall. It has a match." Ruthie made eyes toward Gabby.

Gabby looked down and tucked her necklace behind her shirt.

"Gabby!" gasped Ruthie. "Why did you tuck the necklace behind your shirt?"

"I knew this would happen," said Gabby rolling her eyes.

"I'm confused," said Allie.

"Me too," said Sophie.

"Me three!" said Chrissy.

Ruthie's eyes got watery.

"I got Gabby a birthday present from the jewelry store at the mall, OK?" said Ruthie through her tears. "It's a best friend necklace. I thought we were best friends since I'm Vice President." Ruthie blew her nose into her sleeve. Sophie passed her a Kleenex.

"But I thought we were all best friends," said Emma.

"It's a pretty necklace, Ruthie," said Gabby. "But it makes everyone else feel left out."

"Well, they aren't President and Vice President! They don't get to be best friends. WE ARE!"

Sophie passed Ruthie another Kleenex. Emma opened the Pink Sparkly Notebook.

"Maybe we should read Rule 3. It says: Treat everyone how you want to be treated."

"But I would want someone to give me a half of a best friend necklace," whined Ruthie.

"But what if it makes the other girls feel left out?" Gabby asked.

"Well, they should get a best friend!" said Ruthie crossing her arms and letting out a huff.

"YOOHOOOO!" said a voice coming from below the fort.

Startled, they stuck their heads out the fort window and looked down. Their neighbor, Ms. Margot, was standing at the end of the slide holding a plate of cookies.

"Hi, Ms. Margot!" the girls said in unison.

"Hi, girls! I thought about you all today and wanted to bring you a treat. Also, I don't mean to be a snoop, but I couldn't help but overhear your conversation!"

"We were just talking about best friend necklaces," said Gabby.

"Yes, I heard all of that!" replied Ms. Margot. She was an older lady who lived on the other side of Emma and Allie's house. She wore pink high heels and blue eyeshadow. Her cookies were not the best.

"I know a thing or two about friendship. I have been around a long time, after all!"

The girls came down from the fort and gathered around Ms. Margot.

"Listen up, girls," Ms. Margot began. "Friendship is about more than a heart-shaped best friend necklace. True friendship is about being what I like to call," she left a long pause, "heart friends!" Ms. Margot's eyes got real big and she patted her heart.

"What are heart friends?" asked Sophie, scrunching her nose.

"Heart friends know who you are on the inside and love you just as you are. They help each other when one is having a bad day and laugh with each other when one is having a good day!"

"I get it!" said Mia. "It's being a friend to someone the way you want them to be a friend to you! Just like Rule 3 says!"

"Exactly!" said Ms. Margot. "Ruthie, do you understand now why the necklace you gave Gabby made your other friends feel left out?"

Ruthie looked down at her shoes and shrugged her shoulders. "Yes, ma'am. I guess so." Ms. Margot gave Ruthie a hug. The other girls joined in.

"Doggy darn it! I'm sorry!" said Ruthie. "Ms. Margot is right. We are all best friends!"

"Or better yet," said Emma, "Heart friends!"

ACTIVITY

The Best Way to Make Up After a Fight with Your BFF

Let's face it, girls. Conflict is a part of life. It's not something to hide from or pretend isn't there. Learning to make up when a friend gets their feelings hurt is one of the best ways to be a good friend and will prepare you for the future! Here are some tips on how to deal with conflict together. Remember: Treat each other the way you want to be treated! It makes the world a better, happier, and more loving place for everyone!

1. **Don't pretend:** If your feelings are hurt the worst thing you can do is pretend they aren't! Go to the person who hurt your feelings and tell them how what they did made you feel. Try to stay calm and assume the best about them...they are your friend after all! If they don't listen to you or choose to be unkind, take another friend or adult with you and try again!

2. **Listen and be respectful.** Let them explain why they did what they did. Try not to use words like "you always..." or "you never..." deal with the present issue. Not the past!

3. **Forgive:** Forgiveness is a superpower! Tell the person who hurt your feelings that you forgive them. That means that you won't bring up what they did or said or treat them differently. If you hurt someone else's feelings, be sure to ask them to forgive you for how you made them feel.

THE MISSING PINK SPARKLY NOTEBOOK

8

Emma scribbled in the Pink Sparkly Notebook. Gabby and Mia peered over her shoulder, laughing and whispering.

"What are you writing in the Pink Sparkly Notebook, Emma?" asked Ruthie.

"Just things," said Emma with a sly smile. "Secret club things."

"Like what kind of secret club things?"

"You will find out later!" Emma slammed the notebook and hid it behind her back.

"But I'm the Vice President!" said Ruthie. "I should know about secret things!"

"Not secret things that involve you!" said Mia.

"You shouldn't have said that," said Gabby making wide eyes at Mia.

Mia looked down at the green grass and plucked a handful of blades. She started counting them and tried to change the subject. But it was too late.

"Are you writing mean things about me?" gasped Ruthie. "I'm going to tell my mom!"

"No!" said Gabby. "We are not writing mean things about anyone. We are just making plans and you don't need to see them yet!"

Ruthie crossed her arms and let out a deep breath to let everyone know she was upset. Ruthie was not convinced. Especially after what happened with the heart-shaped best friend necklace. But the other girls never thought about what happened with the best friend necklace anymore. Forgiveness and friendship does that kind of thing.

Ruthie stood up, dusted grass off her shorts and skipped over to where Allie and Sophie were dancing and counting the beats to the music blaring from their speaker.

"Hey, Allie and Sophie!" Ruthie called out above the music. Her mood was peppy and her voice loud.

"Yeah?" they replied. Allie and Sophie didn't stop dancing.

Ruthie continued shouting over the music, "Do you think you could pretty please with a cherry on top go see what Emma is writing in the Pink Sparkly Notebook?" Ruthie batted her eyes and softly tapped her foot on the grass with her arms crossed.

Sophie and Allie stopped dancing and looked at one another. Then they looked at Ruthie.

"We can't," they said matter-of-factly and picked right back up where their dance moves left off.

Ruthie's smile turned into a frown. "Why not?" She was yelling now.

"Because we said we wouldn't break the rules," said Sophie as she swung her ponytail side to side to the beat. It was part of the dance.

Ruthie tapped her foot harder against the grass until it turned into a stomp.

"I promise you will be happy if you don't know," shouted Emma across the yard.

Ruthie whipped around toward Emma, Gabby, and Mia. She started toward them, stomping with each step until her stomps turned into a run.

"I want to know RIGHT NOW!" she cried as she lunged forward to snatch the Pink Sparkly Notebook off Emma's lap.

Gabby grabbed the notebook before it was too late. Ruthie crumpled to the ground, the soft grass breaking her fall. She stood up, let out a sob, and ran into her house and slammed the door. The girls looked at each other. They knew who was about to find out about the secret scribbles in the Pink Sparkly Notebook.

"Something terrible happened!" exclaimed Emma the next afternoon when the girls gathered at the fort. "This morning, I went to get the Pink Sparkly Notebook from the secret spot and it was gone!" Emma kept the notebook in a secret spot no one knew about — or so she thought.

The girls gasped. Emma stood before her friends with a frantic look on her face and told them they needed to find the notebook.

"Does anyone know where the Pink Sparkly Notebook might be?" asked Gabby.

No one said a word.

"That's too bad!" said Ruthie. "I guess that's what you get for writing things about me I couldn't see!"

The girls rolled their eyes.

"It's not what you think it was!" sighed Mia.

"We have to go look for it!" said Emma. "We have important plans inside!"

The girls gathered in the fort and drew a map of Cherry Blossom Place. It would help them in their hunt for the Pink Sparkly Notebook.

"Where was the last place you saw the notebook?" asked Mia.

"Well, in the secret spot," said Emma.

"Where is the secret spot? You're gonna have to tell us," Ruthie replied.

Emma took a deep breath. "Gosh, I really don't want to tell!"

"If you want us to help, you're going to have to tell," said Gabby.

Emma pointed to the big oak tree next to the fort. "The tree over there has a hole in the trunk big enough for the Pink Sparkly Notebook and I always put it inside." Emma led the way as the girls walked toward the oak tree. "See? Here's the secret spot," said Emma. "It's low enough to reach inside and big enough so it doesn't get wet in the rain and stuff."

"That's genius!" said Ruthie.

The girls looked at Ruthie. They all thought the same thing: Ruthie took the notebook.

"I did not take the notebook! I pinky swear!" said Ruthie.

"You sure wanted to know what we were writing in it yesterday," said Mia. "How do we know you didn't take it?"

"I didn't take it! You can go check in my room!"

"We believe you," said Sophie. Sophie turned to the other girls and continued, "Why would Ruthie tear up all the paper inside?" Sophie pointed behind the tree. "See? All the notebook paper is torn into tiny pieces!"

Ruthie ran toward the paper and picked it up. She tried to piece the scraps together. All Ruthie could see were some hand-drawn balloons and the letters "R-T-Y."

"R-T-Y is NOT a word," she said. "This makes no sense." She sat down on the grass and pulled her knees close to her chest. "Now I will NEVER KNOW what you were writing about me!" she cried. Sophie gave her a piece of torn paper and Ruthie wiped her tears with it.

The Backyard Girls decided to make a Missing Pink Sparkly Notebook poster. Gabby drew a picture of the notebook and wrote, "Have You Seen Our Pink Sparkly Notebook?" at the top. Chrissy sprinkled glitter and sequins around the border of the poster. At the bottom, Gabby wrote: Reward paid in cookies, brownies, and gum.

The girls went to every house on Cherry Blossom Place with their poster and asked their neighbors if they had seen the Pink Sparkly Notebook. No one had seen it but hoped the Backyard Girls found it soon. They went to Matt Miller's house last.

"Sorry," said Matt. "I haven't seen your stupid notebook. Probably got eaten by a coyote." The girls gasped.

"I guess I can always buy a new one," said Emma

as they started back to the fort.

"But all of our plans were inside!" said Mia.

"We can remember most of them, right?" asked Gabby. Emma and Mia shrugged their shoulders and looked down.

"Hey, where is that music coming from?" asked Allie as they approached Ruthie's house.

"And why does it smell like cookies and cake?" asked Chrissy.

The girls zigzagged up the driveway toward the backyard. The music grew louder as they turned the corner. Ruthie screamed, cupped her hands over her mouth, and jumped up and down. She looked like she just won the Miss America Pageant.

"I GET IT NOW! R-T-Y WAS MEANT TO SAY PARTY! The secret scribbles in the Pink Sparkly Notebook were plans for my BIRTHDAY PARTY!"

Ms. Sandi stood outside the fort holding a birthday cake on a platter. There were balloons and a piñata, and music from Ruthie's favorite Disney movies played on the speaker. Allie and Sophie performed the dance they made up the day before.

Emma, Gabby, and Mia looked at one another and then at Ms. Sandi.

"Ms. Sandi, how did you know we were planning a birthday party for Ruthie?" asked Emma.

"Well, Ruthie told me you were writing secret things in that Pink Sparkly Notebook of yours. So, I took it upon myself to see just what you were writing."

"How did you know where to look?" asked Gabby.

"Oh, I know all about the tree and the hole. And I was happy to see that you were making plans for a birthday party for my Ruthie. So, I went ahead with your plans and added some of my own. See?"

"Yes, ma'am, we see," said Mia. "But why was all the notebook paper torn up? With all of our plans written on it?"

Ms. Sandi looked down at the cake and tapped her foot. "Well, I had to give you girls something to do while I set up all of the party decorations!"

Ms. Sandi handed Emma the Pink Sparkly Notebook. Emma was relieved, but she decided then and there to keep the notebook in her backpack for now on.

The girls were a little disappointed they didn't get to surprise Ruthie with a party themselves, but Ruthie didn't seem to mind.

"I'm sorry for thinking you were meanies," said Ruthie. "Now I know that you just wanted to surprise me!" The girls hugged. It was another magical day on Cherry Blossom Place.

ACTIVITY

How to Make Your Own Pink Sparkly Notebook

If you have your own Backyard Girls Club you definitely need your own Pink Sparkly Notebook! Remember: It doesn't have to be pink! It can be any color you want. It also doesn't have to be sparkly! Create a club notebook that is as unique as you are.

Here's what you need to create your own:

1. A notebook, binder, or stack of colored paper in your favorite color or colors. If you create your notebook out of a stack of colored paper, punch holes in the paper and tie it together with ribbons, twine or whatever you like!

2. Sparkles, sequins, stickers, ribbons….decorate your notebook with anything you find that makes you smile.

3. Markers, colored pencils, colorful tape and glue will help you create a notebook that you will (hopefully!) never lose!

~*~*CLUB notes~*~*

BACKYARD
~GiRLs CluB~

THE LEMONADE STAND

9

"Ow! Ow! Ow!" yelped Allie as she skipped down the driveway barefoot. Sophie counted how many seconds it took until Allie leaped off the sizzling pavement onto the grass. Everyone else ate icy pops and watched.

Allie jumped onto the cool grass right as Sophie counted to 22.

"UGH! My icy pop melted!" Mia complained. "I only got three licks."

"That's because you didn't eat it in one bite," said Ruthie. "Let me show you."

Ruthie unwrapped an icy pop, stuffed the whole thing in her mouth and ate it in one big bite. Strawberry dripped down her mouth. Chrissy told her sister she looked like she was wearing red lipstick that she put on in the dark. Everyone laughed. Soon, everyone had red, purple, pink, and green mouths - and brain freeze!

Their giggles soon turned to silence. It was official. They were bored. Ruthie cleared her throat.

"OK," she began. "We need to think of something fun to do. It's too hot to sit out here and do nothing. We are melting like these icy pops."

Then they heard it. The sound of a foot pounding the pavement, the crunch of gravel and the "vroom" of wheels.

"Wassup?!?!?" Matt Miller announced as he dropped his scooter on the sidewalk and walked toward where the girls sat cross-legged on the grass.

"We were just deciding what fun afternoon activity we are going to do next," said Ruthie. "And why, may I ask, are you here?"

"That's cool," Matt replied. "I just thought I'd come down and get an icy pop. I saw you eating them from across the street."

Emma pulled an icy pop out of the cooler and handed it to Matt.

"You have to…" Mia started to tell Matt how he should eat his icy pop so he wouldn't have the same melting problem. But Matt unwrapped the icy pop and ate it in one bite before Mia could finish. She was impressed.

"By the way, I'm good at coming up with ideas too, you know," said Matt.

"Well, how about we let you decide what we do next," said Gabby.

"How about a lemonade stand?" said Matt. "Make a little moolah, sit under an umbrella?"

The girls looked at each other. It sounded fun. They knew how to make lemonade because Ruthie and Chrissy's grandmother taught them how when she came for her visit earlier in the summer.

"We could do that," said Ruthie. "But what if we had a lemonade stand competition? Whoever makes the most money wins."

"What do we win?" asked Matt.

The girls looked at each other.

"Whoever wins gets to make the backyard like a beach for the day tomorrow," Ruthie said. "And the loser has to serve the winner the whole day."

The girls thought that was the best idea Ruthie ever had. They giggled as they pictured Matt bringing them soda and serving them icy pops on a tray.

"But you can only sell lemonade," said Gabby. "No glittery pencils like you do at school."

"Yeah, and you have to have a sign and a table," said Mia. "We will set up our lemonade stands across the street from each other at the end of the cul-de-sac so we can get the traffic on the main road."

"It's on!" said Matt. He jumped on his scooter and zoomed back to his house to prepare for battle.

***

The girls found the perfect spot on the sidewalk to set up a pink umbrella and 7 lounge chairs. They decorated a table with streamers, garland, and balloons and wore matching sunglasses and hats. They made five gallons of Ruthie's grandma's famous lemonade. Mia said they should keep some in a cooler and one gallon in a pitcher on the table.

Gabby made a sign that said: Ice, Cold, Lemonade 25 cents. It was written with a green and yellow glitter marker. Sophie, Allie, and Chrissy even came up with a cheer for the girls to do as cars drove by:

"Ice Cold, Lemon-ade!

Drink a glass,

In the shade!

WHOOO!"

The girls peered over their sunglasses at Matt Miller's lemonade stand.

"Our is way better," observed Ruthie.

"That's the grocery store brand lemonade!" shouted Mia across the street to Matt. "You didn't even make that!"

"It's lemonade, ok?" said Matt. "That's all that matters." Matt's mom was throwing a dinner party that night. She bought several gallons of lemonade from the grocery store. Matt figured she wouldn't mind if he borrowed a few, or all of them, to sell.

The girls stuck their tongues out at Matt. Matt rolled his eyes and lined his gallons of lemonade up on a table he carried from his garage.

"Ok, we are going to sell lemonade for the rest of the afternoon," directed Gabby. "Whoever makes the most money by the time the street lights come on wins!"

After a few minutes, Ruthie whispered something to the other girls. Matt watched out of the corner of his eye. The girls giggled. Matt was curious and a little bit suspicious.

Matt watched Emma, Allie and Mia walk up the sidewalk carrying a gallon of lemonade and knock on Mr. Bob's front door. They poured the lemonade in a cup and gave it to Mr. Bob. Mr. Bob fidgeted around in his pockets and gave the girls a quarter. The girls said thank you and walked to the next house.

Matt watched with frustration as the girls went door to door and sold their lemonade while the others served customers who drove by and stopped. Sophie even had the idea to serve lemonade to customers at their car window.

"NOT FAIR!" Matt raised his voice and pounded his fists on his card table, shaking the gallons of lemonade and toppling over his cups. He watched the girls make their second sale at Ms. Margot's house — who bought three cups of lemonade.

"That's 75 more cents!" said Gabby. She wrote it down in the Pink Sparkly Notebook with a smile.

"We never said you had to stay at the table and sell your lemonade, Matt," shouted Gabby. "We just said whoever sells the most wins. This was your idea, after all." She turned and waved her sign advertising their lemonade to a big red truck as it drove by.

Matt sat down at his card table and looked at his several gallons of lemonade. A few minutes later, he picked up a single gallon and made his way toward some men repairing a roof on the house across the street.

"You guys look thirsty!" said Matt.

"Hey, kid! What you got there?" asked one of the workers.

"Lemonade!" said Matt. "And not just any kind of lemonade. The best lemonade."

"How much?" asked one of the men who said his name was Bruce.

"Twenty-five cents for a cup, Mr. Bruce."

Bruce and the other workers went to their truck and pulled out their wallets. That's when Matt had an idea.

"Or," began Matt. "You can buy the entire gallon for $1.50."

"That'll do," said Bruce. "Hey, guys," Bruce said, motioning to the other workers. "This kid is selling lemonade by the gallon. How 'bout we help him out?"

The workers, about 10 in all, walked toward Matt.

"We'll take 10 gallons," said Bruce. "It's a blazer out here today."

Matt multiplied $1.50 x 10 in his head. He was glad he was good at math.

"That'll be $15.00, sir!" said Matt.

Bruce gave him a crisp $20 bill. "Keep the change, kid."

Matt beamed and stared at his $20 bill. He couldn't believe it! He had just sold all of his lemonade at once. Matt walked across the street toward his table and picked up two more gallons. Bruce and the other construction workers helped Matt carry them back to their construction site.

The Backyard Girls watched with frustration.

"Uggghh! But how did he...?!" whined Ruthie. She stomped her foot.

Matt waved his $20 bill toward the girls and sat down behind his lemonade stand. He kicked his feet up on the table and dreamed about the comic books he would buy with his money. A few moments later, a yell interrupted his thoughts:

"MATTTTTTTTTTTTTTTT MILLER COME HOME THIS INSTANT!"

Matt's eyes grew big. It was his mom.

"She must have noticed her missing lemonade," he thought. The girls watched as Matt jumped on his scooter and started down the road toward the grocery store.

The girls giggled and sold their lemonade until the street lights came on. The next day, the Backyard Girls had no trouble coming up with an idea. Matt Miller had plans, too.

ACTIVITY

How to Have Your Own Lemonade Stand

Having your own lemonade stand is a fun, easy way to make your neighbors smile! Here's how you can build your own. You can be as creative as you wish with your signs and set-up, but these are some easy ideas to get you started!

What you need:
- Lemonade — The easiest to use is the lemonade you just add water to and mix!
- Paper cups
- A cooler full of ice
- A table
- Chairs
- Poster board + Markers
- A box to keep your money
- Umbrella... to keep you cool!

You can decorate your table with streamers, balloons, paper cut outs of lemons or even colorful banners! Make sure you make a sign big enough for people to see when they drive by. You can even make up a cheer, like the Backyard Girls love to do! Set your table up in a place where you will be able to get lots of traffic, but make sure you keep it a safe distance from the street. Ask an adult to help you and make sure you make someone in charge of the money!

THE BACKYARD GIRLS PARADE

PARADE!

10

It was the most depressing day of the year: The last day of summer vacation. School started the next day, and the Backyard Girls huddled at the fort. They sat on the top level, watching the clouds form different shapes in the sky.

"That cloud looks like a giant Santa," said Sophie. She was pointing to a puffy, white cloud that did look exactly like Santa — curly white beard and all.

The other girls agreed that the cloud did look a lot like Santa. Ruthie said she couldn't wait until Christmas because it meant two weeks off school.

"School starts tomorrow and you're already talking about Christmas vacation?" asked Mia.

Ruthie reminisced about how Santa brought her the fort last year.

"That was the happiest day of the year," said Ruthie. "And is why we've had so much fun, of course."

"This is the saddest day of the year," Emma declared. "I have the nervous noodles." It was the same feeling she had the day she moved to Cherry

Blossom Place. "I don't feel so good. Maybe I can take a sick day!"

"When did you eat noodles?" asked Allie. "Mom never cooks noodles." Emma rolled her eyes and returned to staring at the sky and the puffy white clouds.

"O, o, o, o! Look at that cloud!" Sophie was pointing right above the fort. "It looks like a float! Like in a parade!"

That's when it happened.

An idea sparked like fireworks inside Gabby's mind.

"What if we made the last day of summer the most fun day of the year?" said Gabby.

"How do we do that? I would rather be in school!" said Mia.

"Let's have a parade!" Gabby exclaimed. Excitement erupted on all of their faces.

"Fabulous idea, Madam President!" said Ruthie. "Everybody go to your house and look for anything we can use for a parade!" directed Ruthie. "Meet back here at the fort in an hour!"

The girls returned with all kinds of things for their parade:

Ruthie found a box of balloons from her birthday party. "It says 100 count," she said. "Let's blow them all up!"

Sophie and Gabby brought poster board and markers. "We can make signs like they have on football Game Day. My Dad always laughs at the signs people make," said Gabby.

"We have glitter pens, too," added Sophie. "I also brought my Mom's Fire Truck Red lipstick for us to wear!"

Emma and Allie brought speakers and an iPod to play music, as well as tutus and batons.

"I have a lot of tutus," said Allie. "Everybody can wear one!"

Emma told the girls they had plenty of music for the parade and made a playlist of their favorite songs.

The Backyard Girls got to work blowing up balloons and making signs. They wore their tutus and Fire Truck Red lipstick. Gabby showed them how to twirl their batons and Chrissy brought everyone pom-poms.

But one thing was missing: PEOPLE!

"We have to invite the neighbors!" said Mia. "We can't have a parade without them!"

Gabby had an even better idea: "We aren't going to just invite them to watch! We are going to invite them to be in the parade with us! No one can sit out!"

The Backyard Girls made a line. Ruthie and Gabby led the way lifting their batons in the air.

The music played loud, but the Backyard Girls sang louder. Fairy and Ivey joined in the fun, too. On leashes, of course. Ruthie held a bouquet of balloons and passed them out to the neighbors as they came out of their houses to see what was causing the ruckus.

"Everyone parades!" they said to their neighbors. "No one sits out!"

It became such a sight that the Backyard Girls' parade began to draw a crowd. Which was what they hoped!

The neighbors on Cherry Blossom Place came out of their homes. First, there was one family, then three, then more. One neighbor, Ms. Shelby, held her pet rabbit named Mr. Foo Foo and Ms. Anne and her cat Tabitha joined in. It wasn't long until all the onlookers decided to join the Backyard Girls and their parade.

When the Backyard Girls turned around and saw the neighbors following them down Cherry Blossom Place, they let out a squeal. Songs and laughter rang out from friends and neighbors as they paraded down their street, bringing more people out of their homes. People held balloons. Matt Miller did tricks on his scooter and passed out cups of lemonade. Someone called the news station and people took pictures. The Fire Chief came, too! He drove his fire truck down the street and the firemen tossed out candy. The parade line stretched for two blocks now.

"You girls sure know how to have fun!" the neighbors said.

"You made the last day of summer the best day of the year!" said another.

The Backyard Girls giggled, said thank you, and paraded until the streetlights came on.

ACTIVITY

How to Create Your Own Backyard Girls Club

Whether you live in a house on a cul-de-sac, a house on a regular street, or an apartment building you can have a Backyard Girls Club. Starting your own Backyard Girls Club is easy! Here are the ingredients you need to cook up fun, magic, and more in your neighborhood!

1. **Round up your best neighborhood friends.** If you don't know them, meet them! Use the questions in the first activity in Chapter 1 to get to know the girls who live around you and maybe even invite them over to make some Magic Cookie Bars in Chapter 2!

2. **Pick your place to have your first official Backyard Girls Club meeting.** It doesn't have to be a fort. Just pick a safe place outside. It can be a driveway, the front porch, back porch, or on a blanket in the backyard. Anywhere is the perfect spot!

3. **Vote for your leaders! If you want to have a president, vice president, secretary and treasurer, go for it!** Just remember that being a leader does not mean being bossy! It means serving and loving the Backyard Girls by treating them the way you want to be treated! Pick your Backyard Girls Club leaders based these key words:

   President: Kind to everyone, problem-solver, loves others, good at encouraging
   Vice-President: Supportive, good at helping
   Treasurer: Responsible, good at math (adding and subtracting!)
   Secretary: Neat handwriting, loves to take notes, organized

4. **Create your own Pink Sparkly Notebook.** Use the activity in Chapter 8 to get started!

5. **Come up with your rules and password.** The rules don't have to be strict like at school! Just a few things you want to always keep in mind when you play together!

Most of all... HAVE FUN!

~*~*CLUB notes~*~*

BACKYARD
~GIRLS CLUB~

~*~*CLUB notes~*~*

BACKYARD
~GiRLs CLuB~